Sam and Nate

PJ Sarah Collins

with illustrations by
Katherine Jin

ORCA BOOK PUBLISHERS

Library and Archives Canada Cataloguing in Publication

Collins, P. J. Sarah, 1971–
Sam and Nate / P.J. Sarah Collins; with illustrations by Katherine Jin.
(Orca echoes)

Issued in print and electronic formats.
ISBN 978-1-55143-334-9 (pbk.).—ISBN 978-1-55143-771-2 (pdf).—
ISBN 978-1-55469-705-2 (epub)

I. Jin, Katherine, 1964- II. Title. III. Series.
PS8605.O47S24 2005   jC813'.6   C2004-907255-2

First published in the United States, 2005
Library of Congress Control Number: 2004117324

Summary: The story of a developing friendship between two boys,
told through their school experiences.

Orca Book Publishers gratefully acknowledges the support for its publishing programs
provided by the following agencies: the Government of Canada through the Canada Book
Fund and the Canada Council for the Arts, and the Province of British Columbia
through the BC Arts Council and the Book Publishing Tax Credit.

Design and typesetting by Lynn O'Rourke
Cover artwork by Katherine Jin

ORCA BOOK PUBLISHERS
orcabook.com

Printed and bound in Canada.

21 20 19 18 • 7 6 5 4

For Isaiah.
And thank you, Alison, Curtis, my family
and the inspirational kids at Maple Grove.
—PJ.S.C.

CHAPTER ONE
Letters from the Mailbox Center

Sam and Nate were both new students at Fir Creek Elementary School. Mrs. Licorice, their teacher, put their desks together.

On Monday, when he finished his work, Sam went to the Mailbox Center and wrote Nate this letter:

Dear Nate,
    I like it that you are sitting next to me. When is your birthday? What is your favorite color? What is your favorite mammal?
    birthday _____
    color _____
    mammal _____
From, Sam

And Nate wrote back:

Dear Sam,
   You always listen when I talk and I think you are smart.
From, Nate

P.S. March 14, red, sharks.

On Tuesday Sam read five books in the library before the first bell rang. Nate had a fight with his sister and was late for school. On Tuesday, when he finished his work, Nate wrote Sam this letter:

Dear Sam,
   I like your printing it is very good what is your favorite toy and book. Well bye bye.
   toy _____
   book _____
From, Nate

And Sam wrote back:

Dear Nate,

Did you know that there are nine planets and that Jupiter is the largest? Pluto is the one that is farthest away. Did you know that it takes 365 days for the earth to orbit the sun?

What is your favorite planet? _____
From, Sam

P.S. - I like Lego and mazes

On Wednesday Mrs. Licorice asked Sam to share his ideas more in class. Nate got in trouble for interrupting. On Wednesday, when he finished his work, Sam wrote Nate this letter:

Dear Nate,

Do you know that the earth has a crust, mantle, outer core and inner core? And Nate

do you know that there are four kinds of rocks? I drew a picture on the back of the letter to show you what it looks like when you cut the earth in half.
From, Sam

P.S. – Did you notice that Mrs. Licorice always wears black?

And Nate wrote back:

Dear Sam,
    You should talk more in class sometimes you are too quiet
From, Nate
next to your desk

P.S. - earth

On Thursday Sam took a long time to finish his work even though he said it was easy-peasy. Nate asked Mrs. Licorice if he could change desks, but she said, "Not now." On Thursday Nate and Sam didn't write any letters. But, at lunch Mrs. Licorice found these notes all crumpled up near the Mailbox Center:

Bossy Buster

balloon brain

Mrs. Licorice sent the boys to the time-out chairs. Sam and Nate sat and thought for a long time.

Finally Nate told Sam, "Don't show off so much."

And Sam told Nate, "Don't boss me."

"Okay," said Nate.

"Agreed," said Sam.

And they shook hands and smiled.

On Friday Nate and Sam became friends. They played together, ate together and sat together in school. On Friday, when he finished his work, Nate wrote Sam this letter:

Dear Sam,

    I like you I'm glad we're friends do you want to play tag at recess and do you want to do puzzles instead of letters?
From, Nate

And Sam didn't write back. Instead, he turned to Nate and with a very big smile said, "YES!"

CHAPTER TWO
Wild Animals

On Monday during lunchtime Mrs. Licorice and Mr. Marvel, the janitor, moved everyone's desk.

"We're going to research animals this week," said Mrs. Licorice. "Now find your group and decide what you want to study."

Nate looked at Sam. Sam looked at Nate. Their desks were on the opposite sides of the room! Sam's group had two boys and two girls in it. Nate's group was all girls, except, of course, for Nate.

Sam's group wanted to study something scary.

"Is the flesh-eating virus an animal?" asked Russell.

"No," said Sam. "But did you know that the duckosaurus could knock a T. rex over with its tail?"

Sam's group all agreed that dinosaurs were scary, especially the duckosaurus.

"I'm going to be a paleontologist some day," said Sam.

"Me too!" said Russell.

Nate's group mostly wanted to study something from the zoo.

"How about penguins?" said Polly.

"How about sharks?" said Nate. "The hammerhead or great white?"

"How about snakes?" said Polly.

"If you like dangerous reptiles," said Nate, "we could study the Gila monster."

Emma scrunched up her nose. "We want to study monkeys."

"I'm allergic to sharks and snakes," said Iris, with a sniff, "so I vote for monkeys too."

Nate's group chose monkeys, three against one. Nate asked Mrs. Licorice if he could change to the dinosaur group, but she said, "No."

On Tuesday Nate's group looked at books about monkeys. They wrote down five facts.

"Not as boring as I thought," Nate said to himself.

On Tuesday Sam's group looked for facts about the duckosaurus. They checked five books, but they couldn't find one single fact.

"Are you sure the duckosaurus is real?" asked Russell.

"Yes," said Sam, looking down. "It had a beak like a duck and laid eggs the size of grapefruits. I saw it on a video."

"I guess we could write that down," said Russell, tapping his pencil on the table. "But Mrs. Licorice told us we had to study a dinosaur that's in these books."

During recess Sam and his group met by the swings to draw dinosaurs. Emma, Iris, and Polly were chasing Nate. They needed a silverback male for their gorilla game.

On Wednesday Nate's group looked at more books about monkeys. They wrote down ten facts.

"Monkeys are actually quite interesting," said Nate.

On Wednesday Sam's group checked ten more books but couldn't find anything about the duckosaurus.

"Are you sure the duckosaurus isn't made up?" said Russell, squinting at Sam.

"Mostly sure," said Sam, kicking his shoe. "It ate two hundred pounds of plants a day and could live almost a hundred years. I saw it at the museum."

"Well, that's two more facts," said Russell. "But all the other groups have more stuff written than we do."

On Wednesday Sam and his group met by the logs to look at Sam's dinosaur model. Nate was hiding from Emma, Iris and Polly, who wanted him to hunt with them for termites like chimpanzees do.

On Thursday Nate's group went on-line with Mr. Keeper, the librarian, and printed fifteen more facts.

On Thursday Sam's group went on-line with Mr. Keeper and couldn't find one single fact about the duckosaurus. But they did find facts about hadrosaurs, which were sometimes called duckbills. They had a beak like a duck, laid eggs like grapefruits, ate lots of plants and could live a long time. But they could only knock over a T. rex if they were very, very lucky.

"Not so scary," said Russell, looking at Sam.

"Sorry," said Sam, as his face went red. "I got mixed up."

"That's okay," said Mr. Keeper. "Now you can go back and check your dinosaur books for hadrosaurs facts. I know they are full of them." Then the librarian walked away.

"I have a better idea," said Russell to the group. "We should kick Sam out, and he should study shrimp because he's small."

During recess Sam's group met by the logs to look at Russell's real-life dinosaur bone. That is, all except for Sam, who walked slowly to the slide and started to crawl under it. And that is where he found Nate.

"What are you doing here?" asked Sam.

"Hiding from my group," said Nate. "What are you doing here?"

"Hiding from my group," said Sam.

Then Nate told Sam about his problem. "I like learning about monkeys, but I don't like being chased like one."

And Sam told Nate about his problem. "I made a mistake about hadrosaurs, and Russell said I should study shrimp because I'm small."

"Russell the muscle," said Nate.

Sam smiled, then thought for a minute. "Well, maybe Russell should study slugs and learn something."

"Or study cats because he's a copycat," Nate said with a giggle.

"Yeah," said Sam. "Or maybe…"

"Yeah?" said Nate.

"Maybe I should just tell Russell that everyone makes mistakes and I said sorry, and he can't kick me out of our group because he's not my boss."

"And I could tell Emma, Iris and Polly that I don't want to be chased around all recess. When I say, 'No' to playing Monkeys, I mean N-O!"

Sam stood up. "I'm going to march over to Russell right now."

"And I'm going to find those girls and let them know I'm serious," said Nate.

"Only…"

"Yeah?"

"How about you come with me?"

"And then you come with me?"

"Okay," they said at the same time. And then they smiled.

The ~~Duckosaurus~~ Hadrosaurs Group
mostly by Russell (Sam, Luka, Nisha too)

1. thE ~~duckosaurus~~ hadrosaurs could
   knock over a T-REX. if it was very
   very very very very lucky
2. it has a beak like a Duck
3. it has eggs that are Very large like
   grape ~~froots~~ fruits
4. it can eat two hundrEd pounds of
   plants in 1 day
5. the ~~duck-o-saurus~~ hadrosaurs lives
   100 years

Sam should go in the shrimp group.

No I shouldn't.

facts about ~~sharks tigers~~ monkeys page 1
by Nate and Iris and Emma and Polly

1. apes do not have tails monkeys do
2. the howler is very loud it is the loudest
3. the silver back male gorilla is the boss
4. chimpanzees like termites they use a stick to poke them out of the dirt then eat them ~~yuck~~
5. the gibbon are good singers
6. ~~marm~~ marmoset is the smallest monkey
7. apes have bigger brains than monkeys they are smarter
8. monkeys who live in trees have longer arms
9. ground monkeys are fast
10. it is very ~~danj danerour~~ dangerous to sleep on the ground. except for gorillas
11. tree top ape s go on the ground maybe two times in one year.
12. it is lots of work to eat leaves you need another stomach

13. only chimps eat other monkeys

14. monkeys and apes like to groom each other

15. gorillas like to live on old volcanoes. cool

16. baby monkeys hold onto their mothers they don't fall off. that is amazing

17. monkeys and apes like to play ~~lite~~ fight

18. monkeys and apes like to live in groups they have there own territory. they ~~mihght~~ might not get along with other groups

Chapter Three
R-E-S-P-E-C-T

One day Sam and Nate decided to ask their parents for the same things: matching green dinosaur knapsacks, lunch bags and caps.

Nate said, "Please, Mom? I'll be nice to my sister, infinity times ten."

And Sam said, "Dad, I finally decided how I want to spend my birthday money."

When Sam got his green dinosaur knapsack, lunch bag and cap, Nate was mostly happy for him. When Nate finally got his green dinosaur knapsack, lunch bag and cap, Sam was thrilled.

Each day they brought their knapsacks to school; at recess they wore their caps, and during the noon hour they carried their lunch bags.

"We're almost dinosaurs," said Sam.

"Almost twin dinosaurs," said Nate.

Then Nate and Sam decided to wear only green to school.

"Now we're really dinosaurs," said Nate.

"Pretty close," said Sam.

Then Sam and Nate decided to eat only green food like sushi, green Kool-Aid and kiwis.

"We're really Jurassic," said Sam.

"We're prehistoric," said Nate.

Nate and Sam wanted to be twins in everything. Then one Monday morning during music, Mrs. Licorice taught the class a new song called "R-E-S-P-E-C-T." It was about treating others the way you want to be treated.

"This song rocks," said Nate.

"It makes my toes tap," said Sam.

Then Mrs. Licorice asked, "Who would like to do the actions for this song?"

The whole class waved their arms. That is, the whole class except for Sam, who put his hands under his seat.

"We'll need seven children to be the seven letters, R, E, S, P, E, C and T. If you want to be a letter, write your name on a piece of paper and I'll pull the seven names from this basket," said Mrs. Licorice.

"I REALLY want to be a letter," said Nate, and he rushed to write his name, big and scribbled, on a piece of paper.

NATE

"I don't know," said Sam, and he put his finger to his forehead.

"We're twins aren't we? It'll be double-the-fun if we both get picked."

Sam nodded slowly and wrote his name on a tiny piece of paper in very tiny letters. Then he scrunched it up into a teeny tiny ball.

Mrs. Licorice started to pick names from the hat. "Let's see.

"R — Polly.

"E — Russell.

"S — Emma.

"P — Marco."

"OH NO!" said Nate.

"Whew!" said Sam.

"E — Alexander.

"C — Iris.

"And T — Sam."

"Ahhhh!" said Nate.

"Ahhhh!" said Sam.

"Now, I'll need my letters to practice during lunchtime all this week," said Mrs. Licorice.

"Like every lunchtime?" asked Sam.

"Like today?" said Nate.

"Like right now," said Mrs. Licorice. "Everyone else should go straight to the lunchroom."

Polly, Russell, Alexander, Emma, Iris and Marco found their lunch bags and returned to the carpet. Sam and Nate shuffled to the cloakroom for their dinosaur bags filled with green grapes and apples, green ketchup, green cookies, cucumbers and green rice.

"I really wanted to do the actions with you," said Nate.

"I really don't want to do the actions at all," said Sam.

Nate walked toward the door while Sam shuffled to where the others were sitting, eating their lunches. Sam wasn't a tiny bit hungry, so he just sat there.

"Now, I'll give everyone a letter and when I say your letter, hold it up nice and high," said Mrs. Licorice, stretching her arms to the ceiling. "Like this, ta-da!"

The children smiled. That is, all except for Sam, who was still clutching his green dinosaur bag.

"Okay, here we go," said Mrs. Licorice. "Everyone stand up.

"R — hold it higher, Polly.

"E — slow down, Russell.

"S — steady Emma.

"P — don't cover your face, Marco.

"E — try not to wiggle, Alexander.

"C — be careful, Iris.

"T — oops, Sam? Be careful!"

But Sam had already dropped his lunch bag and his letter.

"Pick me," said a small voice from the corner.

"Pardon?" said Mrs. Licorice, turning around.

The voice made no answer. Mrs. Licorice turned back to the children.

"Now, let's try the same thing, but this time do a little twirl before you hold up your letter, like this." Mrs. Licorice turned around and held up her hands, "Ta-da!"

The children laughed. That is, all except Sam, who still looked terrified.

"Here we go!" said Mrs. Licorice.

"R — nice twirl, Polly.

"E — that's right, Russell.

"S — much better, Emma.

"P — you've got it now, Marco.

"E — right on, Alexander.

"C — that's it, Iris.

"T — oops, Sam? Watch out!"

But Sam had tripped and fallen to the floor.

"Uh-oh," said a loud voice behind the couch.

Mrs. Licorice walked over to the couch and peeked over.

"Nate!" she said. "What are you doing hiding there?"

"I, uh, want to help my twin."

Mrs. Licorice looked at Nate for a moment, and laughed out loud. "Well, I could sure use a helper. Would you like to join us? We were just going to listen to the music before we put the actions and music together."

Nate nodded and sat down next to Sam. Nate opened his green dinosaur lunch bag. He pulled out his green grapes and started to nibble on them.

Then he said, "You know, if you watch a spot on the floor, you won't fall over."

"Really?" said Sam.

Nate nodded. "That's the trick," he said. "Keep your eyes down."

Sam opened his green dinosaur lunch bag. He

pulled out his green apples and started to nibble on them.

When the music stopped, Mrs. Licorice said, "Everyone up. Let's try the actions again.

"R — good, Polly!

"E — great, Russell!

"S — wonderful, Emma!

"P — excellent, Marco!

"E — terrific, Alexander!

"C — nice job, Iris!"

And this time Nate joined her:

"T — Way to go, Sam!"

CHAPTER FOUR
Something Fishy about Mrs. Licorice

One Monday Mrs. Licorice announced that it was Whale Week. "We're going to study whales all week long."

Sam smiled at Nate. Nate smiled at Sam.

"Do we get to study sharks too?" asked Nate.

"No, Polly," said Mrs. Licorice. "Sharks are not whales. Whales are mammals, and sharks are fish."

The children all laughed, all, that is, except for Mrs. Licorice, Sam and Nate.

"I'm not Polly," said Nate, as his face went purple. "I'm NATE!"

"Oh, I'm so sorry, Nate," said Mrs. Licorice. "Where is my mind today?"

When the class stopped being silly, they got right to work. They measured how long the blue whale would be if it swam in the hallway. They used tape to show that it was about one hundred feet long.

"That's bigger than a car," said Nate.

"That's bigger than two buses," said Sam.

"What a fun day!" said Nate, as the bell rang.

"Except that Mrs. Licorice never mixes up our names," said Sam.

"So what?" said Nate.

"Hmmm," said Sam, putting his finger to his forehead.

On Tuesday, the class learned about the two types of whales: toothed and baleen.

"The main difference between them is how they eat," said Mrs. Licorice.

"Why do you have red bits in your hair?" interrupted Nate.

"Oh, do I?" said Mrs. Licorice, as she ran her fingers through her hair. "I've been busy painting

at home." She smoothed her black skirt and said, "Do you think red is a nice color?"

Many of the children nodded their heads.

"I like it too," said Nate.

"Hmmm," said Sam. "There's something fishy going on."

On Wednesday the class studied whale behaviors and watched a film. They learned that when a whale breaches, it jumps out of the water.

"Whales are excellent communicators," said Sam.

"Yeah, they can send messages a long way without cell phones or computers," said Nate.

"Hmmm," said Mrs. Licorice. She was staring at the ceiling.

Nate looked up too. "What are you thinking about?"

"I wonder if the mail arrived yet."

"Earth to Teacher, are you there?" asked Russell.

"Oh! I must be daydreaming," said Mrs. Licorice.

The children all laughed. All, that is, except for Sam.

"Hmmm," said Sam. "Something is definitely fishy."

On Thursday the class studied ocean habitats and where exactly each kind of whale lives. Then they painted shoeboxes and started cutting out pieces for their whale habitat dioramas. When it was time to clean up, Mrs. Licorice told the class not to put the paint away.

"Yippee! Are we painting again after lunch?" asked Nate.

"No," said Mrs. Licorice. "I'm going to paint a box so I can take a diorama home as well."

"Oh," said Nate. "Does Mr. Licorice like whales too?"

"Not especially," said Mrs. Licorice.

"Hmmm," said Sam. "Something is definitely fishy, and I don't know what it is."

On Friday morning Mrs. Licorice divided the class into two teams. Then she changed her voice and pretended to be a famous TV person.

"Good morning," she said. "And welcome to the

Whale Quiz Show. My name is Suzy Smart and I'm your host. Here is how we play."

"It's a bit like tic-tac-toe," said Nate.

Halfway through the game Sam started to giggle. At first it was quiet. Then his giggles got louder and louder. He bit his lip, but he couldn't stop giggling.

"Sam, what's so funny?" said Mrs. Licorice in her real voice.

Sam got really quiet. He whispered something into Nate's ear.

"Sam is wondering why Suzy Smart is wearing two different colored shoes!" said Nate, pointing at his teacher's feet. Mrs. Licorice was wearing one black shoe and one blue one.

All the children laughed, including Sam and Nate. Mrs. Licorice laughed too. Her face turned red, but she kept laughing.

Finally the laughter stopped. "I was going to tell you this afternoon," Mrs. Licorice said, "during our whale party, but now seems like a good time."

"Finally," said Sam.

"I'm… Well, I'm going to have a baby," said Mrs. Licorice, her eyes shiny. "Very soon, Mr. Licorice and I are going to have a child."

"But you don't look different," said Nate.

"Yeah, you're not even big like a whale," said Russell.

"Well, I'm not actually having the baby," said Mrs. Licorice. "The baby is coming to us from Brazil."

"Interesting," said Sam.

"Yes," said Mrs. Licorice. "We're adopting a little girl named Maria who is already one year old. Maria needs a home, and we have a home to give."

"Oh," said Polly. "Math time will be really loud with a baby in the room."

"Oh," said Iris. "Can we hold Maria if we finish our work early?"

"No," said Mrs. Licorice. "When Maria comes, she's going to need someone to take special care of her at home. And that someone will be me."

The class got very quiet.

"Who will be our teacher?" said Nate.

"Suzy Smart!" said Mrs. Licorice, with a laugh. "For now, anyway. Let's finish our game."

for fun whale facts

by Nate and Sam together

these are the parts of a whale:

blowhole dorsal fin flukes eye ear flippers
the biggest whale is the blue whale it is over
100 feet long

the two types of whales are toothed and
baleen the toothed whales have one blow hole.
and the baleen whales have two

baleen whales are bigger than toothed whales

whales don't lay eggs but fish do

fish tales go side to side. whale tails go
up and down

when whales jump out of the water it is called
breaching

spy hopping is when a whale pokes its
head out of the water and one way whales
communicate is by slapping their flukes and
flippers

CHAPTER FIVE
The New Teacher

One Friday Sam and Nate's class had a good-bye party for Mrs. Licorice.

"Thank-you for the lovely surprise," she said. When the last bell rang, Mrs. Licorice stood at the door. "Hug or handshake?" she asked each student. Sam and Nate were the last ones to leave.

"Handshake," said Sam. He held out his small hand and looked away.

"Hug," said Nate. He wrapped his arms around Mrs. Licorice's waist.

"You're going to love your new teacher," said Mrs. Licorice, with a sniff. "He used to teach high school and he's very interesting."

Sam looked at Nate. Nate looked at Sam.

"He?" said Sam.

"High school?" said Nate.

On Monday morning when the bell rang, there was no sign of the new teacher. By the time the second bell rang, the classroom was really quite noisy.

"Yippee," said Russell. "The new teacher is sick."

Just then Mrs. Focus, the principal, entered the room followed by a very tall, skinny man wearing a red polka-dot tie and carrying a stack of papers.

"Quiet, children," shouted Mrs. Focus. "This is Mr. Tangent. He's going to be your teacher for the rest of the year. I know you'll show him our famous Fir Creek Elementary good manners."

"Good morning, Mr. Tangent," said the children.

"Oops," said Mr. Tangent as he dropped his pile of work. Sam and Nate, who were the closest to the mess, crawled over to help pick the papers up.

"I guess I'm just N-E-R-V-O-U-S," said Mr. Tangent to Mrs. Focus.

"Let me know if you need anything," she said and left the room.

"How about more C-O-F-F-E-E?" said Mr. Tangent.

Sam looked at Nate. Nate looked at Sam.

"This is going to be F-U-N," said Nate.

"And a little W-E-I-R-D," said Sam.

Mr. Tangent took a long time to take attendance. At ten o'clock Mr. Keeper, the librarian, knocked on the classroom door.

"Excuse me, but the children are twenty minutes late for their library time."

"Oops," said Mr. Tangent as he adjusted his tie. "I guess I F-O-R-G-O-T. Line up, kids."

"A bit different from high school?" asked Mr. Keeper.

"The children are so T-I-N-Y!"

Mr. Keeper laughed as he led the class away.

Sam looked at Nate. Nate looked at Sam.

"I guess he doesn't know we can S-P-E-L-L," said Sam.

"N-O-P-E," said Nate.

After recess Mr. Tangent gave the children some pictures to color. Sam and Nate finished in five minutes.

"What should we do now?" asked Nate.

"Color another one," said Mr. Tangent.

"And then?" said Sam.

"Draw."

At eleven o'clock Ms. Goodwin, the school secretary, knocked on the classroom door.

"Mrs. Focus said to hurry to the gym. You're late for the special assembly."

"Oops," said Mr. Tangent as he adjusted his collar. "I must have misplaced my C-H-A-R-T. Line up, kids."

Mr. Tangent ran with the children to the gym.

Sam puffed at Nate. Nate puffed at Sam.

"This isn't N-O-R-M-A-L," said Sam.

"I M-I-S-S Mrs. Licorice," said Nate.

After the assembly, Mr. Tangent let the children have free time. Most of the kids went straight to the musical instruments, and the classroom got very loud and very messy. At ten to twelve Mr. Marvel, the janitor, knocked on the door, but he had to do it twice because no one answered right away.

"I didn't see you downstairs," said Mr. Marvel. "Just wanted to remind you that your gym time is up in ten minutes."

"Oops," said Mr. Tangent as he pulled at his hair. "My M-I-S-T-A-K-E."

When the class got to the gym, the lunch bell rang. The children had to go all the way back upstairs to get their lunches.

Nate looked at Sam. Sam looked at Nate.

"That's I-T!" said Nate.

"We have to make a P-L-A-N," said Sam.

After they ate, Sam and Nate sat under the slide. They talked and wrote in Sam's notebook. By the time the bell rang, they were feeling much better. They raced back into the school and up the stairs to the classroom.

Mr. Tangent was already there. He was sitting at Mrs. Licorice's old desk with his head down. He looked very big and very tired.

Sam looked at Nate. Nate looked at Sam.

"Excuse me, Mr. Tangent?" said Sam.

"Yes?" said Mr. Tangent as he looked up. Nate noticed that his polka-dot red tie was all crooked, and his hair was all messy.

"Here is where Mrs. Licorice keeps our schedule," said Nate, opening the cupboard.

"And here are our class rules," said Sam, pointing to the wall.

"We only get free time when the class has earned enough points for good behavior," said Nate.

"Thank-you, boys," said Mr. Tangent, as he started to smile. Sam noticed he had a kind face.

"But there's more," said Nate.

"Here is where we keep our work," said Sam, pointing to some baskets. "We can do all kinds of things: science, math, reading, writing, art, social studies and..."

"You little kids sure are smart!" said Mr. Tangent.

"And one other thing, sir," said Nate. "We can S-P-E-L-L."

Mr. Tangent stood up, surprised. "You can?"

"Y-E-S," said Nate.

"That's wonderful," said Mr. Tangent, with a laugh. "There's so much I can T-E-A-C-H you too."

"O-U-T-S-T-A-N-D-I-N-G," said Sam. And then he giggled.

Chapter Six
The Messy Mix-Up

When Mr. Tangent told Sam and Nate's class that they were going to study weather, Nate jumped up and down.

"Did you know that my dad is the weatherman for CUTV? I know all about weather," he said. "We talk about it every morning and every night."

"A class expert," said Mr. Tangent. "How helpful."

"Can we go outside for our lessons?" asked Russell.

"Soon," said Mr. Tangent. "But not yet."

Mr. Tangent taught them all about the atmosphere. Then he accidentally dropped a globe on his foot and yelped out loud. It was noisy after that, but the kids still learned that there is no air in space.

"Then there can't be any sound either," said Sam.

"My dad knows all about high pressure and low pressure," said Nate.

"Can we go outside now?" said Russell.

Mr. Tangent showed the kids a demonstration of the water cycle. Then he accidentally slipped on a puddle of water on the floor. It was chaotic after that, but the kids still learned that precipitation is a fancy name for rain.

"Dew is formed from moisture in the air," said Sam.

"My dad says that rain is measured in milliliters," said Nate.

"Now can we go outside?" said Russell, when the nurse told Mr. Tangent that nothing was broken.

Mr. Tangent bought new posters about the different types of clouds. Then he accidentally mixed up all the names. It was confusing after that, but the kids still learned that there are four main types of clouds.

"The cirrus clouds are the highest," said Sam.

"My dad can tell what kind of clouds are in the sky even if he has a blindfold on," said Nate.

"I think it stopped raining," shouted Russell.

Mr. Tangent showed the kids a video about snow crystals. Then they worked in groups to answer questions. Mr. Tangent was really quiet that day, but the kids still learned that snowflake patterns are unique.

"There aren't two the same," said Sam.

"My dad gets to go in helicopters and be on TV," said Nate.

"Will we ever go outside?" begged Russell.

"Tomorrow," said Mr. Tangent. "We will also have a class party in the afternoon to celebrate weather."

Everyone clapped and cheered.

The next morning Mr. Tangent taught about the wind. The children made pinwheels. Then Mr. Tangent showed the children pictures of some damage caused by windstorms.

"My dad says that hurricanes, cyclones and tornadoes can be deadly," said Nate with a frown.

"That's very true," said Mr. Tangent. Then he taught everyone about the Beaufort Scale. "It's a system that indicates wind strength. The Beaufort Scale goes from zero to seventeen. When it's very calm out, the wind strength is at zero. When there is a hurricane, the wind strength is at seventeen."

"My dad says there has never been a hurricane in our province," said Nate.

"Hurricanes can only happen where it is warm and flat," said Sam. "And we're near the mountains."

Mr. Tangent opened a wooden box and took out a metal machine. "I have an instrument here that measures the wind strength. It's a beautiful day, not a cloud in the sky, so why don't we try this out with our pinwheels?"

"Finally!" shouted Russell.

"Why do the numbers on that instrument go past twenty?" said Sam. But nobody heard him. They were too busy pushing for the door.

When the children got outside, they ran to make their pinwheels spin. Mr. Tangent held the metal instrument up above his head.

"Look," said Polly. "It says the wind strength is at one."

"No," said Nate. "It's moved up to three."

"It's at six," said Iris.

"No, nine," said Marco.

"Eleven!" yelled Emma.

"Fifteen!" shouted Alexander.

"This is not possible!" interrupted Nate. "My dad says..."

But nobody heard him. The dial on the instrument was rising to...

"Seventeen!" screeched Russell.

"Hurricane! Hurricane! Hurricane!" screamed everyone, that is, everyone except for Mr. Tangent, Sam and Nate, who were busy scratching their heads.

"Oh," said Mr. Tangent, with a laugh. "My mistake, again—this thing has nothing to do with the Beaufort Scale. It just powers this small fan here."

But only Sam and Nate heard him. The other children were racing for the school.

"Hurricane! Hurricane! Hurricane!" they screamed up and down the stairwells, scattering their pinwheels on the steps.

"Come back!" said Sam and Nate.

"Be quiet! Calm down!" shouted Mr. Tangent.

But the class would not be quiet.

"Hurricane! Hurricane! Hurricane!" they screamed up and down the hallways, knocking over the recycling bin by the main door.

"Come here! Be quiet! Calm down!" cried Mr. Tangent, waving his arms, before he fell onto the grade five's papier-mâché village display.

"Huuuriiiicaaaaane!" bellowed Russell into the office.

Mrs. Focus told him to sit in her time-out chair. Then she turned on the PA.

"There Is No Hurricane Coming. I Repeat. There Is No Hurricane Coming. Would The Children In Mr. Tangent's Class Please Return

To Their Classroom Immediately," she said.

The children all returned to their room, still excited and completely out of breath.

"There will be no party this afternoon," said an embarrassed Mr. Tangent after he explained the mix-up. "During lunch I want you all to tidy up the mess we made in the school. And in the afternoon, to help you calm down, I will give you a weather test."

Everyone moaned and groaned.

"But…" said Sam.

"That's not fair," said Nate. "Sam and I tried to tell everyone."

"It was your mistake, Mr. Tangent," said Russell, crossing his arms.

After lunch Mr. Tangent was about to hand out the test when there was a knock on the classroom door.

Mr. Tangent turned the knob and swung the door open. In walked Mrs. Licorice and Maria. Behind them stood a smiling man with black hair and glasses.

"Dad," yelled Nate, running to hug him.

"Have you already started the party?" asked Mrs. Licorice.

"You're right on time," answered Mr. Tangent, as he dropped the pile of test papers back onto his desk.

Everyone cheered and clapped.

"Oh, thank-you, Mr. Tangent!" said Polly, hugging him around the knees.

"We knew you weren't unfair," said Iris.

"Before we start the party, though," said Mr. Tangent, "Mrs. Licorice and I want everyone to get into a sharing circle."

"What's that?" asked Nate, holding his dad's hand.

"It's when we all take turns sharing our most memorable discovery this term. For example, I discovered that I enjoy teaching elementary school much more than high school."

"And I discovered that kids of all ages are a lot of fun," said Mrs. Licorice, smiling at Maria.

"I discovered that a howler monkey can make more racket than my baby brother," said Polly.

"And I discovered that there's a proper way to announce an emergency," said Russell.

"I discovered that it's not so scary to stand up in front of the whole class and be a T," said Sam, "Especially with help."

Sam looked at Nate. Nate looked at Sam.

"And I discovered that even imaginary hurricanes can cause a lot of damage," said Nate.

And then everyone giggled.

A VERY SMALL BIBLIOGRAPHY

Eyewitness: The Visual Dictionary of Dinosaurs. Dorling Kindersley Limited: London, 1993.

Eyewitness: Whales. Dorling Kindersley Limited: London, 1993.

Gelman, Rita Golden. *Monkeys and Apes of the World.* Franklin Watts: New York, 1990.

Sam and Nate is **PJ Sarah Collins**'s first published book. She enjoys family life, teaching in Vancouver and studying children's literature. When asked to describe herself, the author said, "I aspire to be like Sam and Nate in their simplicity and joy of life, but I'm often more like Mr. Tangent." For more information, visit pjsarahcollins.wordpress.com.

Katherine Jin created the interior illustrations for *Sam and Nate* in pencil. She created the cover in watercolor. She lives in London, Ontario.